© 1997 Owl Records Ltd
Published by Geddes & Grosset, an imprint of
Children's Leisure Products Limited,
David Dale House, New Lanark, ML11 9DJ, Scotland,
for Owl Records Ltd, Dublin, Ireland

First printed 1997
Reprinted 1998, 1999, 2000, 2002, 2003, 2004

ISBN 1 85534 775 X

Printed and bound in Slovenia

Oisín
and Tír na nÓg

Retold by Reg Keating
Illustrated by Heather McKay

Tarantula Books

Oisín loved poetry, music and song. When he was twenty years old, he was the best-loved poet in Ireland. People came from every province just to hear him read and sing.

One day, a beautiful young maiden came to hear his poems.

She had bright blue eyes and long golden hair. Her skin was as clear and fresh as a rose petal.

H er dress was made of the finest silk. Her cloak was embroidered with emeralds and jewels. She wore silver shoes with golden buckles.

She rode the finest white horse that was ever seen in Ireland.

Her name was Princess Niamh. She had travelled very far from the land of Tír na nÓg.

Tír na nÓg was a magical land far out beyond the western sea.

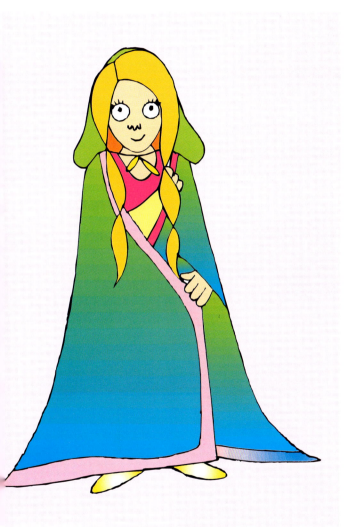

In this land, no one ever grew old. It was a land where the sun never set and the rain never fell. Tír na nÓg was the land of eternal happiness.

Day after day, Niamh listened to Oisín's poems and songs. Soon, she fell in love with him.

Oisín fell in love with Niamh, and they were both very happy.

S oon the time came for Niamh to return to Tír na nÓg.

She begged Oisín to go with her to Tír na nÓg. She told him he would never grow old and that he would be happy forever.

Because he loved Niamh so dearly, Oisín agreed to go with her to Tír na nÓg.

There was much sadness when the people of Ireland waved goodbye to Oisín and Niamh.

Before long, the great white horse was carrying them off to the west.

With just a few galloping strides, they reached the coast at Connemara. Then the horse galloped over the tops of the waves and off out to sea.

When Oisín looked back, Ireland had disappeared below the horizon.

In no time at all, they reached the magical land of Tír na nÓg.

The King and Queen of Tír na nÓg welcomed Oisín to his new home.

They had heard much about Oisín and his poetry. They were happy to have him as their son-in-law.

The next day, Niamh and Oisín were married.

The wedding feast was the finest ever seen. Everyone in Tír na nÓg was invited.

Just as in Ireland, everyone in Tír na nÓg loved Oisín.

Both he and Niamh were very happy.

When one year had gone by, Oisín wanted to visit Ireland one more time. He wanted to see his father, who was Finn mac Cumhall.

One day, Oisín told Niamh of his plan. She was very deeply troubled. She feared Oisín might never return from Ireland.

When Oisín promised he would return, Niamh agreed to let him go.

"Be very careful," warned Niamh, "and do not touch the ground in Ireland. If you do, you will never again return to Tír na nÓg."

When it was time for Oisín to go, Niamh warned him again.

"Do not dismount from the great white horse. He will bring you back safely to Tír na nÓg."

Niamh was very sad as she waved goodbye to Oisín.

Before long, Oisín and the great white horse were on their way back to Ireland

Once more, they galloped over the top of the waves.

S oon the coast of Connemara came into view.

When they reached Ireland, Oisín could not recognise the land. Everything had changed.

The great plains where Oisín and Finn and the Fianna had roamed were gone. The great Fianna fortresses were in ruins. They were overgrown with briars and brambles.

The people's dress had changed.

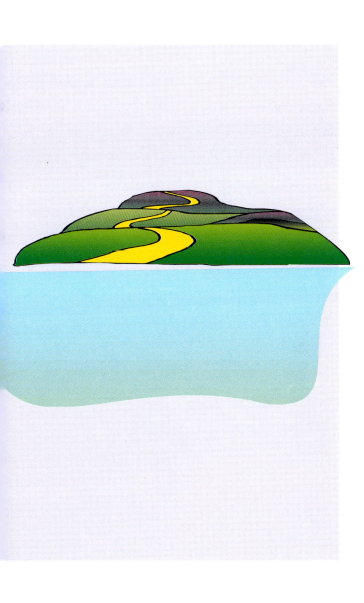

Oisín asked about Finn and the Fianna. "They have been dead for hundreds of years," the people told him.

Then Oisín understood what had happened. One day in Tír na nÓg was the same as a year in Ireland.

Oisín had been away for more than three hundred years.

Sadly, he turned back for Tír na nÓg.

On the way, he met some men struggling to move a heavy stone.

The men asked Oisín to help. Oisín did not refuse.

He reached down from his saddle and picked up the stone with one hand.

The men were astonished at Oisín's great strength.

Suddenly, the saddle girth snapped. Oisín fell from the horse.

The moment Oisín touched the ground he changed.

He was no longer a handsome young prince. Instead, he had turned into a withered old man.

The great white horse took fright. It galloped back to Tír na nÓg and was never seen in Ireland again.

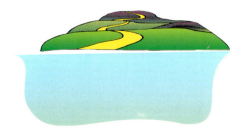